THE USBORNE YOUNG SCIENTIST
STARS & PLANETS

It takes a well-trained eye to read the sky and a wide range of telescopes and probes to study it in detail. Here are just some of the tools astronomers use to look at the universe.

Orbiting observatories like OAO-3 enable astronomers to photograph the stars without having to peer through Earth's murky atmosphere.

A prism splits light into a rainbow of colour called a spectrum. By studying the spectrum of a star's light, astronomers can find out about its make-up.

The 100 m Effelsburg dish near Bonn in Germany is the biggest rotating radio telescope in the world. Such giant 'telescope ears' let scientists probe deep into the universe.

The 66 cm Washington refractor telescope was built in 1862. Astronomers using it discovered the moons of Mars and the companion star of Sirius.

Credits

Written by
Christopher Maynard
Revised text by
Christopher Cooper
Art and editorial direction
David Jefferis
Design assistant
Iain Ashman
Revised edition designed by
John Barker

Scientific advisers
Adrian Berry, FRAS
Kenneth Gatland, FRAS, FBIS
Nigel Henbest, MSc, FRAS
Illustrated by
Michael Roffe, Malcolm English
and John Hutchinson
Copyright © 1991, 1977 Usborne
Publishing Ltd.

The name Usborne and the
device are Trade Marks of
Usborne Publishing Ltd.

Acknowledgements
We wish to thank the following
individuals and organizations for
their assistance and for making
available material in their
collections.
Space Frontiers Ltd.
National Aeronautics and Space
Administration (NASA)
British Interplanetary Society
Royal Astronomical Society

First published in 1977 by
Usborne Publishing Ltd.
Usborne House,
83-85 Saffron Hill,
London EC1N 8RT, England.

Revised edition published 1991
Printed in Italy

**On the cover: Voyager space
probe passing Saturn and its
largest moon Titan, whose
surface is hidden by an orange
haze.**

The experiments

Here is a checklist of the equipment you will need for
the experiments and things to do included in this book.

WARNING:

Never look at
the Sun directly, either
with your eyes or through
binoculars or telescopes.
If you want to observe
the Sun, use the safe
Sun-scope shown
on pp. 10–11.

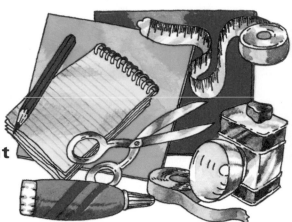

General equipment

Scissors
Sticky tape
Ruler
Chair
Binoculars
Felt pen and pencil
If you can afford it, buy a tripod
to mount your binoculars on. Your
arms will not ache, and the view
will be much steadier.

Special experiments

Looking at the sky (p.6):
Deckchair
This book
Torch or bicycle lamp
Thermos flask
Notebook
Warm clothing

Phases of the Moon (p.8):
Grapefruit
Golfball
Torch

Sun-scope (p.10):
Two sheets of white card
Binoculars

Meteorite craters (p.18):
Plain white flour
Shallow tray
Spoon

Sky-Spy (p.26):
Large sheet of tracing paper
A world atlas
A sheet of white card

Weights and measures

All the weights and measures used in this book are Metric.
This list gives some equivalents in Imperial measures.

mm = millimetre
(1 inch = 25.4 mm)

cm = centimetre
(1 inch = 2.54 cm)

m = metre
(1 yard = 0.91 m)

km = kilometre
(1 mile = 1.6 km)

kph = kilometres per hour
(1,000 mph = 1,609 kph)

kps = kilometres per second

kg = kilogram
(1 pound = 0.45 kg)

1 tonne = 1,000 kg
(1 ton = 1.02 tonnes)

°C = degrees Centigrade
(Water freezes at 0°C and boils
at 100°C.)

Speed of light = 300,000 kps
Light year = 9,460,000 million km

Contents

About this book

Stars and Planets is a beginner's guide to the universe we live in. Its clear text and detailed pictures take the reader on a journey through the familiar sights of the night sky and on to the frontiers of the unknown.

Stars and Planets explains how scientists think the universe began and how Earth, a speck in space, fits into the cosmic picture. Readers will visit the still smouldering crater of a giant meteor strike, see the planets of the solar system, and be shown how matter and energy are sucked into black holes.

It also contains safe and simple experiments that can be done at home with ordinary household equipment. They range from simple illustrations of scientific principles to projects like building a sun-projector.

The universe of stars

Earth and Moon

▲ Here is the Earth and its satellite the Moon. The Earth has a diameter of 12,756 km while the Moon is barely one-quarter as large. The average distance between the two is 384,000 km. Yet this is next to nothing. Even the nearest planets are tens of millions of kilometres away.

The Solar System

▲ The Earth, under the red arrow, is just one member of the solar system. Here, within a space of 11,800 million km, are the Sun, 9 planets, over 60 moons and thousands of asteroids and comets. Beyond is a void of some 40 million million km until the closest star, Alpha Centauri, is reached.

The universe is unimaginably huge. Our planet, Earth, is merely a tiny pinpoint in space. As a planet, it is rather small and unimportant. Next to any one of the millions upon millions of stars in the universe, Earth is barely noticeable at all.

In the bubbles above, the red arrows show the location of Earth. Each bubble shows a bigger portion of the universe, the last taking you to the outer limits of known space.

Astronomers know that the universe is expanding. How and why this is happening are still very much unanswered questions.

In the beginning . . .

▲ The origin of the universe has always been a puzzle. Astronomers now favour the 'Big Bang' theory. They think that the universe began about 18,000 million years ago with a colossal explosion.

▼ At the moment of the Bang, all the material in the universe was packed together in an incredibly hot, dense mass. The explosion ripped it apart.

The Milky Way

Galaxies like grains of sand

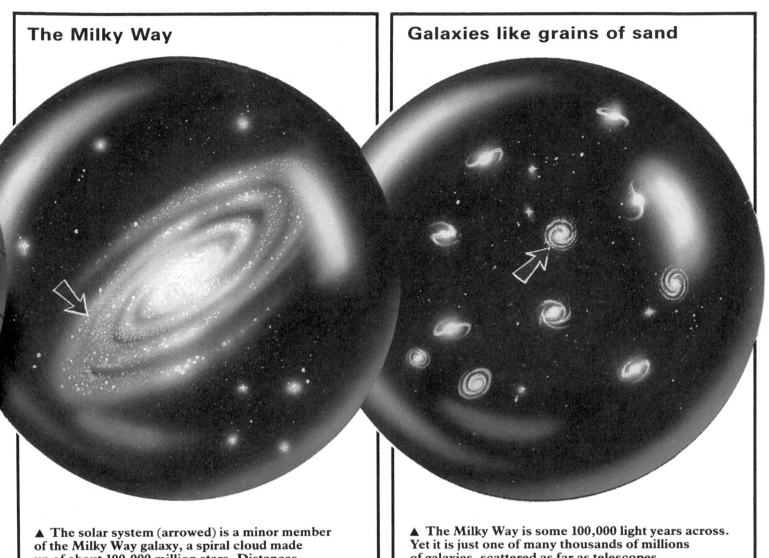

▲ The solar system (arrowed) is a minor member of the Milky Way galaxy, a spiral cloud made up of about 100,000 million stars. Distances in deep space are vast so they are measured in light years. One light year is the distance light travels in a year, 9·46 million million km.

▲ The Milky Way is some 100,000 light years across. Yet it is just one of many thousands of millions of galaxies, scattered as far as telescopes can see. They have been spotted up to 15,000 million light years away. Yet the actual size of the universe is somewhat larger than this.

The expanding universe

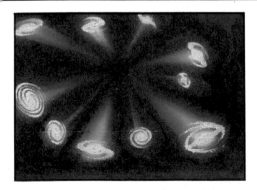

▲ Out of this material the galaxies, stars and planets were formed. But the force of the Bang persists. The universe is still expanding and galaxies everywhere are whizzing apart.

In 1842, the Austrian scientist Christian Doppler showed why the sound of approaching and receding objects was different.

Movement causes the sound waves in front of a moving object to be compressed. The ones behind are spaced out.

The Doppler effect also holds true for light. Light waves from a receding star are spaced out, making the light take on a reddish colour. This light change is called the red shift — all the distant galaxies have a red shift, proof that the universe is expanding.

▲ Hear the Doppler effect in action! Look up at a jet plane and note how the sound changes from a high whine to a low roar as it goes overhead. This is the 'sound' version of the red shift.

Looking at the sky

Two types of telescope

The first telescopes were made in the early 1600s. They were refracting telescopes using lenses to collect light. In 1671, Isaac Newton built the first reflecting telescope. It used a mirror to collect the light.

The large lens in the front of a refracting telescope is called the objective. It collects light rays and bends (or refracts) them to form an image inside the telescope.

Refracting telescope

This diagram shows the path of light rays in the telescope.

Reflecting telescope

This small flat mirror reflects the collected light to the side of the telescope.

The eyepiece picks up the image from the flat mirror. This type of reflector is called the Newtonian focus after its inventor.

The rear lens is called the eyepiece. It magnifies the image for the astronomer to look at.

This diagram shows the path of light rays in the telescope.

The concave mirror collects and reflects light back up the telescope's body.

All you need to look at the sky

Amateur astronomers can have as much fun as the professionals. You need an atlas of the stars and a pair of binoculars. Even your naked eyes will do: with them you can see as many as 3,000 stars on a clear night.

From a comfortable spot outdoors you can chart and log the stars and planets. With luck, you might spot a meteor.

Many comets, such as Alcock in 1959 and Ikeya-Seki in 1965, have been first spotted by amateurs searching with binoculars.

A comfortable deckchair is the heart of an amateur observatory.

You can plot planets and stars with this book.

You need a small torch to read the sky charts at night. Dim the light with red cellophane as shown on p.25.

Ever since Galileo turned his telescope to the sky in 1609, astronomers have been improving the instruments with which they study the stars.

Nowadays, most large telescopes are really 'super-cameras' as film is much more sensitive to dim light than the human eye. Special devices help boost the faintest starlight to a clear strong image.

Stars not only give off visible light, but also emit radio and other waves that are invisible to the human eye. Special methods are used for "photographing" them.

▲ The largest optical telescope today is the 6 m reflector at Mount Semirodniki in the Soviet Union. It can gather starlight 10,000 million times fainter than the brightest star in the sky. It could detect a candle 25,000 km away.

Invisible astronomy

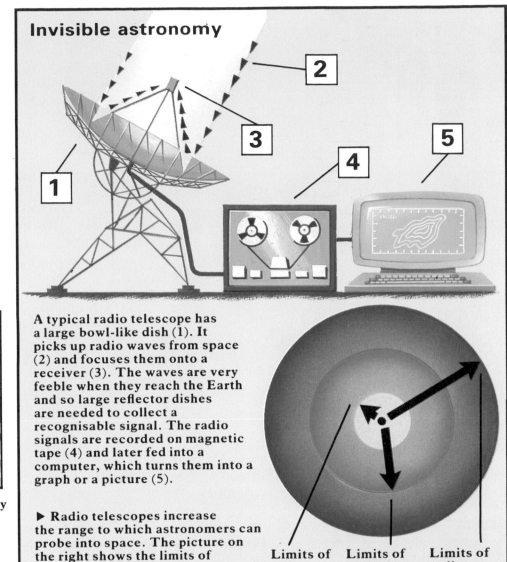

A typical radio telescope has a large bowl-like dish (1). It picks up radio waves from space (2) and focuses them onto a receiver (3). The waves are very feeble when they reach the Earth and so large reflector dishes are needed to collect a recognisable signal. The radio signals are recorded on magnetic tape (4) and later fed into a computer, which turns them into a graph or a picture (5).

▶ Radio telescopes increase the range to which astronomers can probe into space. The picture on the right shows the limits of the naked eye and of optical and radio telescopes.

Limits of naked eye   Limits of optical telescopes   Limits of radio telescopes

A thermos flask with something hot to drink will keep away the night-time chill.

Use a notepad and pencil to make notes and sketches during your skywatching.

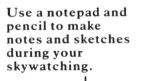

Wear lots of clothes. A pair of old gloves with the fingertips cut off will let you write as well as keep your hands warm.

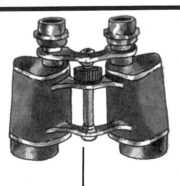

A good pair of 7 × 50 binoculars is better than a cheap telescope. With these, you should be able to see some of Jupiter's moons and details of lunar craters.

Friendly Face in the sky—the Moon

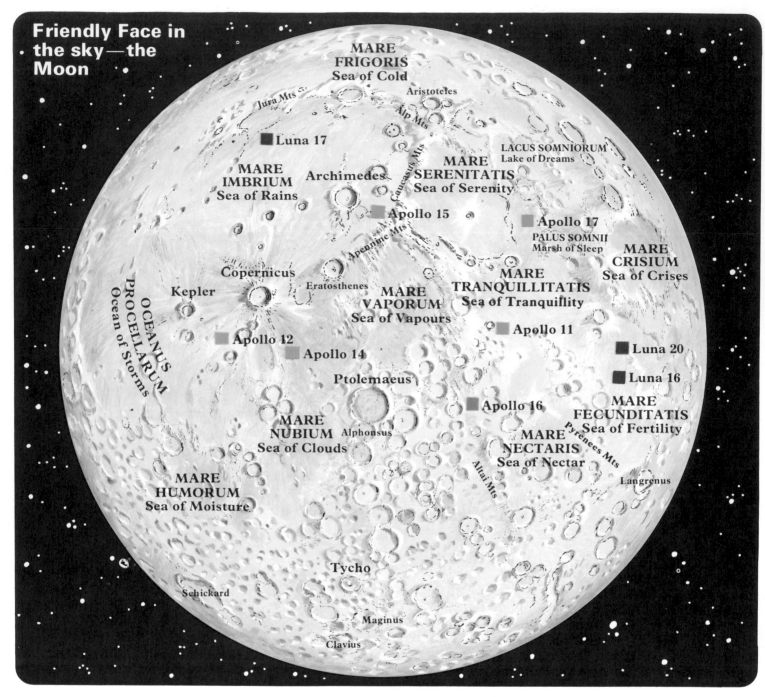

MARE FRIGORIS
Sea of Cold

Jura Mts
Aristoteles
Alp Mts

Luna 17

MARE IMBRIUM
Sea of Rains

Archimedes

Caucasus Mts

LACUS SOMNIORUM
Lake of Dreams

MARE SERENITATIS
Sea of Serenity

Apollo 15

Apollo 17

PALUS SOMNII
Marsh of Sleep

MARE CRISIUM
Sea of Crises

Copernicus

Kepler

OCEANUS PROCELLARUM
Ocean of Storms

Eratosthenes

Apenuine Mts

MARE VAPORUM
Sea of Vapours

MARE TRANQUILLITATIS
Sea of Tranquillity

Apollo 11

Apollo 12

Apollo 14

Luna 20

Luna 16

Ptolemaeus

Apollo 16

MARE FECUNDITATIS
Sea of Fertility

Pyrenees Mts

MARE NUBIUM
Sea of Clouds

Alphonsus

MARE NECTARIS
Sea of Nectar

MARE HUMORUM
Sea of Moisture

Altai Mts

Langrenus

Tycho

Schickard

Maginus

Clavius

Phases of the Moon

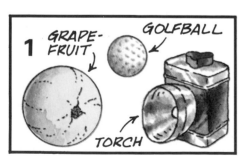

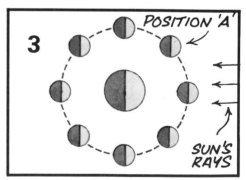

▲ The Moon only shines with reflected sunlight. As it moves around the Earth, we see different parts of its sunny side. For this experiment, you need a torch and two balls—try a golfball and grapefruit.

▲ Balance the torch on a table, or fix it firmly to the back of a chair as shown above. Put the 'Earth' grapefruit and the 'Moon' golfball on the table. Make sure the 'Sun' torch is shining on them both.

▲ Starting from position A shown above, move the Moon around the Earth in a circular orbital path. As the Moon goes around, you will see that the view from Earth goes from shadow to sunlight and then back to shadow again.

Earth's nearest neighbour

The Moon is our closest companion in space and the only one ever to have been visited by Man. Although it is roughly a quarter the size of Earth, the Moon is far less massive. It would take 81 Moons to make up the same weight as Earth.

Gravity on the Moon is quite feeble—only 1/6th as great as on Earth. It is far too weak to hold an atmosphere. As a result, the Moon is a bleak and arid world where temperatures soar to 100°C by day and plunge to a freezing —150°C at night. The Moon's surface is a monotonous expanse of rock and dust.

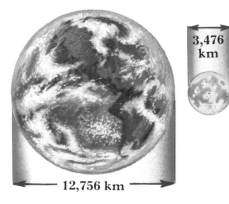

3,476 km

12,756 km

▲ To get an idea of the distance between the Earth and the Moon, trace off the two scale globes shown above onto a sheet of card. Cut out the two circles and knot a piece of string 1.25 m long between them to see the scale distance.

The side we never see

Although the Moon spins on its axis, it always keeps the same face to Earth. It takes the Moon as long to rotate once (27.3 days) as it does to circle the Earth. As the direction of rotation and spin are the same, we never see the other side.

Astronomers had the first glimpse of the far side of the Moon in 1959 when the Russian spacecraft Luna 3 passed behind it and took photographs.

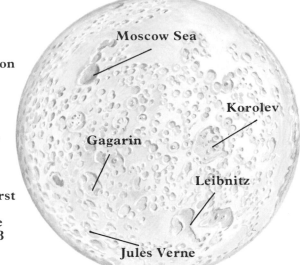

Moscow Sea

Korolev

Gagarin

Leibnitz

Jules Verne

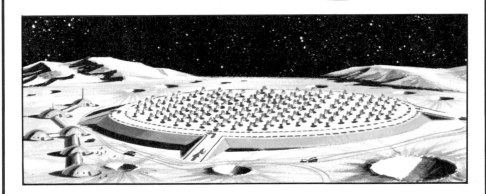

▲ The far side of the Moon is a perfect site for an observatory. Here, optical telescopes would not have to cope with a murky atmosphere. Radio telescopes would use the Moon as a rocky shield 3,500 km thick to protect themselves from the interfering radio waves from Earth. One idea, shown above, is for a vast 'Cyclops-eye' radio telescope to probe into the depths of space.

4

HOW THE MOON LOOKS AT POSITION 'A'

▲ Put the Moon back at position A again, and peer over the top of the grapefruit Earth. If you have got the angle of the light from the torch right, you should see that the lit portion of the golf-ball Moon looks like a crescent.

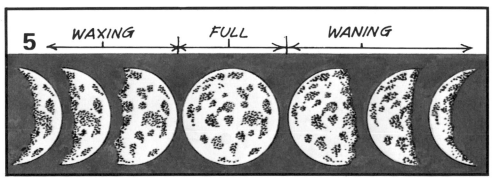

5   WAXING   FULL   WANING

▲ Here are the phases of the Moon as they are seen from Earth. Every 29½ days, the Moon completes a full cycle. It goes through three stages. A waxing Moon is one that is getting larger and brighter. A full Moon is a shining disc in the sky. A waning Moon is getting smaller. When the near side of the Moon is completely in shadow, it is called a new Moon. A crescent Moon in the waxing phase is in the same place as position A in your small-scale experiment model.

The nearest star

The Sun is just an ordinary star. The only reason it looks like a huge burning ball in the sky is that it is millions of times closer to Earth than any other star.

The Sun is the source of all life on Earth. The nuclear reactions in its core provide a steady stream of life-giving light and heat. The Earth receives barely 1/2000 millionth of the total radiation of the Sun. Yet this is enough to warm the planet and provide all the energy for plant and animal life.

Though the Sun uses up four million tonnes of fuel every second, it has enough to burn for a good 6,000 million years yet.

At times, long looping streams of gas called prominences arch up from the Sun. They climb into space at speeds up to 600 kps. Small short-lived prominences are called spicules.

Size of Earth to scale

Dark patches on the Sun's surface are sunspots. They are 1000-2000°C cooler than the surface and so shine less brightly. Sunspots usually appear in pairs. They develop in a few hours and may last for many months.

The surface of the Sun is in continuous upheaval. Swirling gas eruptions called flares often occur with sunspot formations. They release bursts of intense radiation causing magnetic storms that disrupt radio communication on Earth.

▲ The Ulysses spacecraft was launched in 1990 to study the Sun from a new angle. It was due to pass Jupiter 16 months later, so that the giant planet's gravity would swing the probe over the Sun's poles.

Make a safe Sunscope

DANGER—DO NOT LOOK AT THE SUN

Never, ever, look at the Sun through binoculars, telescopes, or even just with your eyes. The strong light can easily blind you. Even smoked glass and sun filters should never be used as they do not block out all the dangerous rays.

1 7x50 BINOCULARS

▲ It is very dangerous to look at the Sun. Filters exist that screen out harmful rays, but it is easier and cheaper to make this sunscope. You need a pair of binoculars — 7 × 50 are ideal — and two sheets of stiff white card.

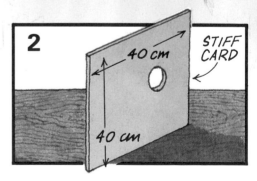

2 40 cm STIFF CARD 40 cm

▲ You need a square of card about 40cm × 40cm. Cut a hole in it as shown above, just big enough to fit one of the binocular lenses. The other lens will not be used in the Sunscope, so you only need the one hole.

Temperatures at the core of the Sun rise to an incredible 15 million °C.

The outer part of the Sun is a 'convection' zone, in which heat is carried outward by hot gases that rise, cool and fall again.

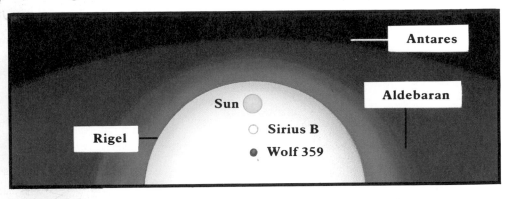

Antares

Sun

Aldebaran

Rigel

Sirius B

Wolf 359

▲ The Sun has a diameter of about 1.4 million km. Its interior could hold more than a million planets the size of Earth. Although this flaming ball of gases looks like the biggest thing in the sky, it is in fact merely a medium-sized yellow star orbiting far out in one of the spiral arms of an average sized galaxy. The picture above shows the Sun compared with some of its stellar neighbours. As you can see, it is a very ordinary star indeed.

The corona is the outer part of the Sun's atmosphere. It can best be seen during a total eclipse when it looks like a glowing halo around the Sun.

The Sun's surface is called the photosphere. Here, the temperature is about 6000°C. Immediately above it is the chromosphere, a thin layer of gases where temperatures fall to 4500°C.

Surrounding the core is a radiation zone of hot gases. They transmit radiation part of the way from the core to the surface.

▲ This picture shows a total eclipse of the Sun. From time to time the Moon passes in front of it and exactly covers the Sun's disc. This is the only time the shining halo of the corona can be seen without special equipment.

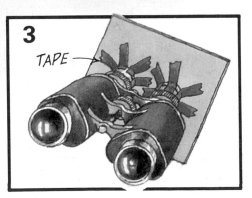

3

TAPE

▲ Lay the card on a table and balance the binoculars on it, making sure that one lens fits over the hole you have cut. Carefully tape the binoculars into place. They must be firm so do not skimp on the tape!

4

SUN'S IMAGE

WHITE CARD

▲ For a screen you need a large sheet of white card. Prop it against a chair at right-angles to the Sun in the sky. Focus the binoculars on infinity and hold them in front of the card. The Sun should appear on it.

5

THE SUN

SUNSPOTS

▲ This is the sort of image you should get quite easily. Move the binoculars backwards and forwards until the image is sharp. With luck, you will see some tiny black specks on the Sun — they are sunspots.

TAKE CARE – if you adjust the Sun's image to make a pinpoint, you may burn the card.

Asteroids

Comets

Sun

Mercury

Venus

Earth

Mars

Jupiter

Saturn

Family of the Sun

The solar system consists of the entire family of planets, moons, asteroids, comets, meteors and swirling dust and gases that circles the Sun. The Sun itself is more than 750 times as massive as the rest of the system combined. Its enormous pull of gravity locks everything within a range of over 6,000 million kilometres into orbit around it.

After the Sun, the most important members of the solar system are the nine planets. The chart below shows you some of the more important facts about each one. Planets' 'days' and 'years' vary because they spin at different speeds and move along in their orbits at varying rates. Pluto, for instance, rotates every 153 hours compared with Earth's rotation time of 23 hours 56 minutes, so Pluto's day is more than six times longer than Earth's.

Facts and figures

Name of planet	Diameter in km	Average distance from Sun in million km	Number of known moons	Time taken to go around the Sun (year)	Time taken to turn on its axis (day)	Speed in orbit around the Sun in kps
Mercury	4,878	57.9	—	88 days	59 days	47.9
Venus	12,100	108	—	224.7 days	243 days	35
Earth	12,756	149.6	1	365.3 days	23 hours 56 mins	29.8
Mars	6,790	227.9	2	687 days	24 hours 37.5 mins	24.1
Jupiter	142,800	778	16	11.9 years	9 hours 50.5 mins	13.1
Saturn	120,000	1,427	19	29.5 years	10 hours 14 mins	9.6
Uranus	52,400	2,870	15	84 years	15 hours 14 mins	6.8
Neptune	50,450	4,497	8	164.8 years	16 hours 3 mins	5.4
Pluto	2,300	5,900	1	248.6 years	6 days 9 hours	4.7

Uranus

Neptune

Pluto

Plotting the planets

The Planets swing around the Sun in regular orbits. From Earth, they seem to move across a narrow belt of sky. This is because the planets circle the Sun in a roughly flat plane, rather like the bands between tracks on an LP record. The only exception is frozen Pluto, the outermost planet which has an angled orbital path.

The planets move through twelve star constellations called the signs of the Zodiac. Once you have spotted the constellations, any extra 'star' will be a planet. The chart below shows where you can see the four brightest planets during the next few years.

Key to the planetary symbols shown below

♀ Venus   ♃ Jupiter

♂ Mars   ♄ Saturn

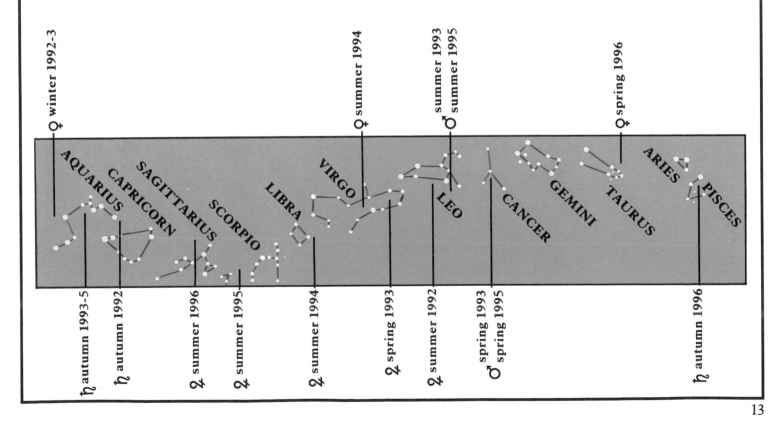

The inner planets

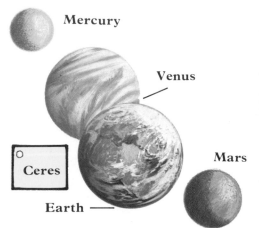

Mercury

Venus

Ceres

Mars

Earth

The four inner planets are the midgets of the solar system. The diagram above shows them all to the same scale, together with Ceres, the biggest asteroid. All are quite dense and, apart from Earth, have barren, rocky surfaces. The features of Earth are softened by the great oceans that cover 71% of its surface.

Only the thinnest of atmospheres exist on Mercury and Mars. As a result there is a great difference between day and night-time temperatures. On Mercury the change can be as high as 400°C. Earth and Venus, however, have shielding atmospheres. Their temperatures are fairly constant. On Earth at the equator, this is about 15°C while most of Venus roasts at nearly 500°C — hot enough to melt lead!

▲ Tiny Mercury is the nearest planet to the Sun which, looming some three times as big as it does on Earth, sears the landscape to a baking 400°C.

In 1974, Mariner 10 passed the planet and snapped the first detailed pictures. They showed a dry rocky surface that was scarred with craters. Instruments on board showed Mercury to have a dense iron-rich core much like that of Earth's.

▲ Venus, the morning and evening 'star', ought to be Earth's sister planet. Its size is almost identical, yet it is a hell-world shrouded by clouds of sulphuric acid and smothered by an atmosphere of carbon dioxide.

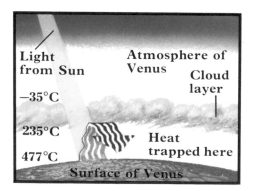

Light from Sun

Atmosphere of Venus

Cloud layer

−35°C

235°C

477°C

Heat trapped here

Surface of Venus

▲ The clouds that blanket Venus trap sunlight like a greenhouse. Light passes through the clouds and heats the surface. The ground radiates infra-red heat waves that are trapped by the atmosphere making temperatures soar.

▲ From nearby space, Earth shines like a blue-white beacon in the sky. Even from the Moon, the brown outlines of the continents, the deep blue of the oceans and the white swirls of the clouds can be clearly seen.

▲ In 1976 two space probes, Vikings 1 and 2, soft-landed on Mars and sent back the first surface pictures. The view above was taken by Viking 2. The horizon is about 3 km away. The fine drifting sand is the result of storms that can rage across Mars.

▲ This picture shows the largest moon of Mars, Phobos, as it might appear from the viewport of a visiting spacecraft as it approaches the red planet. To give you an idea of the moon's size, the crater in the middle is 6 km across. Phobos orbits 6000 km above Mars, circling it three times every Martian day. The other moon of Mars, Deimos, is even smaller than Phobos. It must appear as little more than a bright moving star from the surface.

Lost Planet ?

Orbiting in the 550 million km gap between Mars and Jupiter are tens of thousands of small rocky objects called asteroids. Ceres, the biggest, is only 1025 km across—most are only house or boulder-sized. Astronomers think that the asteroids are the building blocks of a planet which never formed.

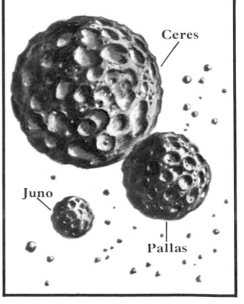

Ceres

Juno

Pallas

The outer planets

Beyond the Asteroid Belt are the outer giants—Jupiter, Saturn, Uranus and Neptune—vast balls of gas circling in the solar system's outer reaches. Beyond them all lies tiny frozen Pluto.

The diagram below compares Earth and the outer planets shown to the same scale.

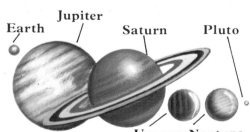

Earth Jupiter Saturn Pluto

Uranus Neptune

▲ **Jupiter is the Goliath of the solar system, having a volume 1,312 times that of Earth. It does not have a solid surface. Jupiter's upper layers are a sea of gases that become a denser liquid and finally a solid near the core. In the visible cloud layers, temperatures average —140°C.**

The oddest feature is the Great Red Spot (shown on the right in the picture above), first seen in 1666. Astronomers think it may be a long-lasting storm raging in the planet's atmosphere.

Pioneer 10 (shown above) photographed Jupiter in 1973; in 1979 Voyagers 1 and 2 returned more detailed pictures. They discovered a faint ring around Jupiter, two new moons, and seven active volcanoes on one of the larger moons, Io.

▼ **Saturn orbits 1,427 million km from the Sun. It is a gas giant like Jupiter, but its amazing rings are what make it really interesting. From Earth, the rings look different from year to year as the planet moves around its orbit. The pictures below show how our view changes.**

The rings are barely a kilometre thick, and are not solid. They are made up of countless small pieces

▲ Uranus is an icy world 2,870 million km from the Sun. Latest studies show that in addition to its 15 known moons (two of which are passing in front of it in the picture above), it has 11 narrow rings, much darker than Saturn's.

▲ Neptune is the last of the giant planets. It is similar to Uranus but slightly smaller. Its two largest moons are named Triton and Nereid. Its cloud layers have been calculated to be at a constant and chilly −220°C.

of rock and ice. In 1980, Voyager 1 discovered that the rings are divided into hundreds of separate "ringlets". The two outermost ringlets are twisted around each other like strands in a rope.

Saturn has at least 19 moons, most of them made of ice and cratered by comet impacts. One has a crater a quarter its own size, and another has been smashed into

by two smaller moons which now share the same orbit. The largest moon, Titan, has a thick atmosphere of nitrogen, and orange clouds which completely hide its surface. Titan's surface temperature must be about −180°C, and astronomers think it may be covered by oceans of liquid methane (the substance we find as natural gas on Earth).

Arrows show position of Pluto

▲ Pluto was not discovered until 1930. Photographs taken on different nights were compared, and one of the "stars"—Pluto—was found to move. Pluto has a moon, Charon, discovered in 1978, which is half Pluto's size.

Meteors and comets

Along with the planets and moons, a great deal of space debris circles the Sun. Most of it is too tiny and distant to be seen from Earth, but at times some of these objects become spectacularly visible.

The smallest are the meteoroids which range from tiny specks to boulder size. They can be seen only when they hurtle into the atmosphere as streaks of light called shooting stars.

Comets are solitary wanderers. A long shining tail announces their arrival whenever they drift in from space and near the Sun.

▲ The picture above shows a meteor as it streaks into the Earth's atmosphere at a speed up to 70 kps. Friction with the air vaporizes most meteors before they get anywhere near the Earth's surface.

▶ Giant meteorites hitting the Earth are very rare, although thousands of tiny meteors burn up in the atmosphere every day. This picture shows what the scene might be like a short time after a huge meteorite hit. Scientists in helicopters hover over and in the newly gouged crater. Luckily, it is in a deserted area.

Meteorite craters

Astronomers call meteors different names according to where they are. A chunk of rock or stone in space is a meteoroid. The same chunk is called a meteor as it falls through the atmosphere. If it actually hits the Earth (or any planet or satellite such as the Moon), it is called a meteorite.

Meteorites can either land in one piece or explode violently. In 1947, a thousand tonnes of fragments from an exploding meteorite rained down on Siberia, digging impact craters that were up to 30 m wide.

FINE PLAIN FLOUR

▲ It is easy to make your own meteorite crater with this simple experiment. The surface of your model planet is a bed of flour. Cover the bottom of a shallow tray with a layer of fine plain flour about 2 cm thick.

SMOOTH OFF WITH RULER

▲ Smooth off the flour with the edge of a ruler. It is important to have a smooth even surface for the experiment to be a success. Place the tray on the floor. Now cover the floor with newspaper for the next step.

Comets—dirty snowballs in space

Comets appear from the depths of space as glowing balls, sometimes with million km tails. A comet's nucleus is a ball of solid particles and frozen ices enveloped by a coma of evaporating gases. A nucleus a few km wide may have a coma of 80,000 km. The Sun's heat and radiation boils away the gas particles from the coma and spreads them back to form a long filmy tail stretching into space.

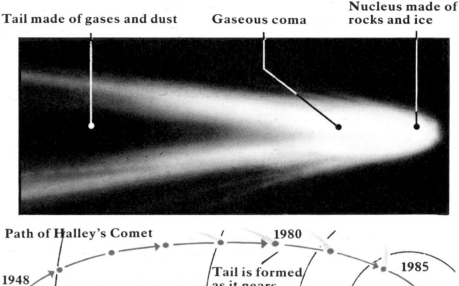

Tail made of gases and dust   Gaseous coma   Nucleus made of rocks and ice

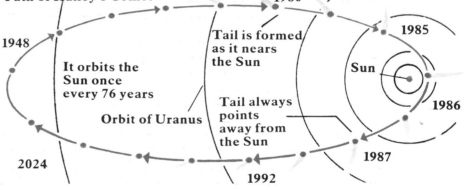

Path of Halley's Comet

1980
1985
1948
Tail is formed as it nears the Sun
Sun
1986
It orbits the Sun once every 76 years
Tail always points away from the Sun
Orbit of Uranus
1987
2024
1992

3 ABOUT 2 m   MAKE SURE YOU CLEAN THE FLOOR!

▲ Climb up on a chair so you are standing directly above the tray. Take a small spoonful of flour, hold it about 2 m above the floor and let the flour drop. Repeat the experiment a few times from different heights.

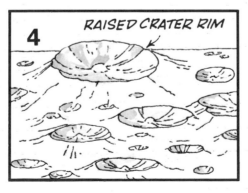

4 RAISED CRATER RIM

▲ The flour ploughs into the tray just like a meteorite hitting the Earth or Moon. You will see that all the mini-craters that are formed in your tray have the same sort of raised lip and sloping sides as real craters.

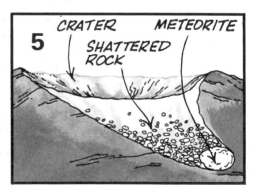

5 CRATER   METEORITE   SHATTERED ROCK

▲ The most famous meteorite crater on Earth was formed 24,000 years ago in the Arizona desert. An iron-nickel meteorite some 80 m wide, blasted into the Earth. It gouged a hole that was 1,265 m wide and 175 m deep.

Star-spotting in the northern sky

There are about 3,000 stars in the night sky that can be seen by the naked eye. Not all are visible at once as only a small part of the heavens can be seen from any single place on Earth.

Only the brightest stars are shown in the map here and on pages 24-25. They are most easily recognised as parts of star groupings called constellations. Most of these were made up by ancient peoples, who imagined pictures of animals and people in the stars. The Plough, part of the constellation of Ursa Major, is easy to spot in the northern sky.

▲ You need the Sky-Spy shown on pp.26–27 if you want to use the sky charts properly. Simply line up the time on the Sky-Spy with the date on the chart. The view inside the oval is what you will be able to see on that night in the sky.

▶ Here are the main constellations of the northern sky. The big numbers on this map link with the pictures on the next two pages.

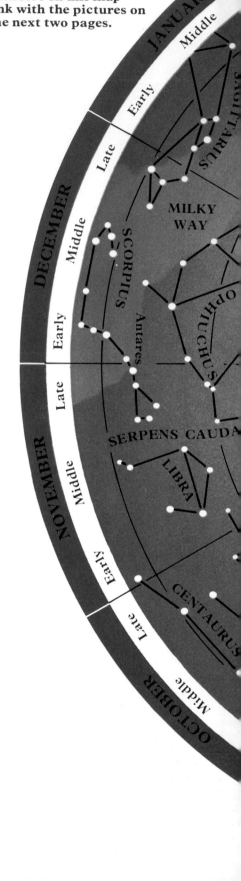

Mapping the heavens

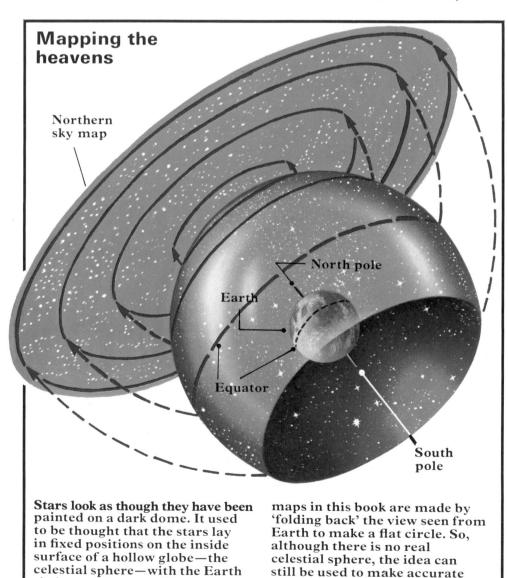

Stars look as though they have been painted on a dark dome. It used to be thought that the stars lay in fixed positions on the inside surface of a hollow globe—the celestial sphere—with the Earth sitting at its centre. The star maps in this book are made by 'folding back' the view seen from Earth to make a flat circle. So, although there is no real celestial sphere, the idea can still be used to make accurate maps of the sky.

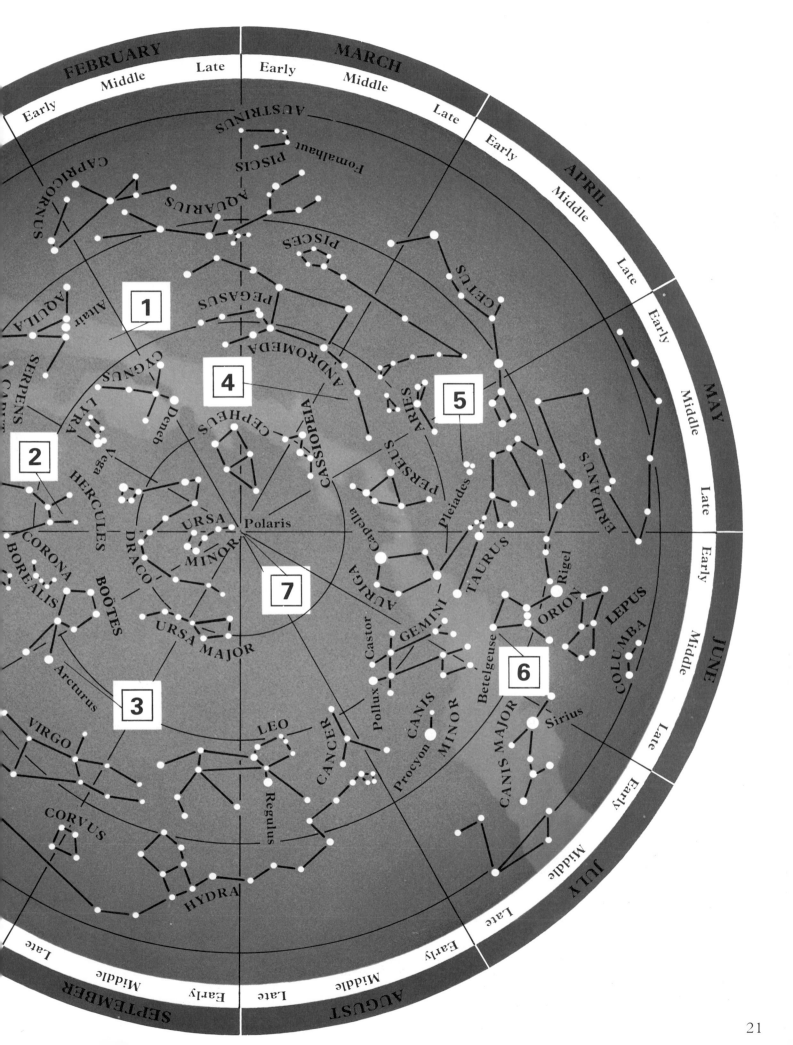

21

Wonders of the northern sky

Not only stars and planets can be seen in the night sky, but also dark nebulae, star clusters, galaxies and shining clouds of heated gas. Many of these sights are too faint to be spotted unaided. They are only visible with powerful telescopes.

Each object in the sky is ranked according to its brightness, which is indicated by a number called its magnitude. Curiously, bright objects are given low numbers; Venus for example is −4.4. Dim objects have high numbers. The faintest object you can see unaided is around magnitude +6.

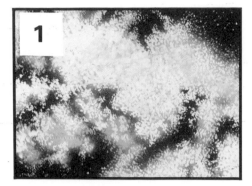

▲ Our own galaxy, the Milky Way, looks like a dim trail of light stretching across the sky. Pictures like the one above show it to be made up of millions of stars so thickly sprinkled that they look like clouds.

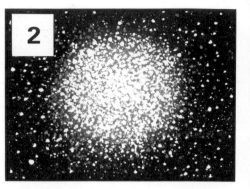

▲ The fuzzy patch in Hercules called M13 is a tight globular star cluster. Here, hundreds of thousands of old dim yellow stars are crowded together. They are packed less than half a light year apart.

▲ The Pleiades are a compact group of stars in the constellation Taurus. They are **about 400 light years away.** The Pleiades are also known as the 'Seven Sisters' since most people can only see seven stars here. However, on a clear night and with very good eyesight, others come into view. Only the sharpest eyes can make out more than fifteen, yet in actual fact there are nearly 400. North American Indians used the Pleiades as a way of testing the keenness of a warrior's eyesight.

The blue-white stars in the Pleiades are 'young'—just a few tens of millions of years old. The Sun is 5,000 million years old in contrast.

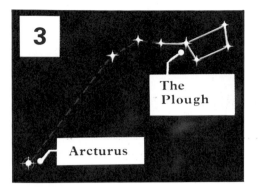

3

The Plough

Arcturus

▲ With the Plough as a guide, draw an imaginary line along the curve of its handle. If you continue the line in the same path, it will cross Arcturus, the fourth brightest star to be seen in the skies.

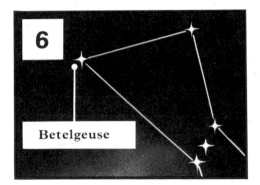

6

Betelgeuse

▲ The constellation Orion can be seen in both northern and southern skies. The picture above shows you how to find Betelgeuse at its top left-hand corner. Betelgeuse is a red-giant star 600 times larger than the Sun.

4

▲ This picture shows the most distant object that can be seen with the naked eye — the Andromeda galaxy. It looks like a faint smudge. The astronomer Edwin Hubble first tried to measure its distance in 1923. It is now known to be two million light years away. Its shape is very like that of our own Milky Way galaxy, complete with spiral arms. The Andromeda Galaxy is almost twice as large as the Milky Way, and it contains three times as many stars.

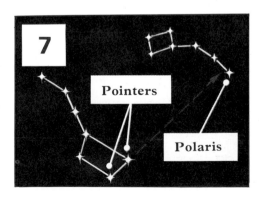

7

Pointers

Polaris

▲ The seven brightest stars of the constellation Ursa Major are called the Plough. A line between the two end stars, the Pointers, runs straight to Polaris when extended upwards. Face Polaris and you always face north.

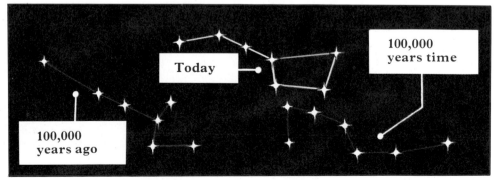

Today

100,000 years ago

100,000 years time

▲ Stars seem to be fixed in the sky. Yet with enough time, movements do become apparent. 100,000 years ago, the stars of the Plough were an unrecognizable jumble. Today, their familiar form is easy to see. In another 100,000 years, the shape will be transformed yet again.

Although stars move at high speeds, they are so far away that any motion is impossible to make out, except with high precision instruments.

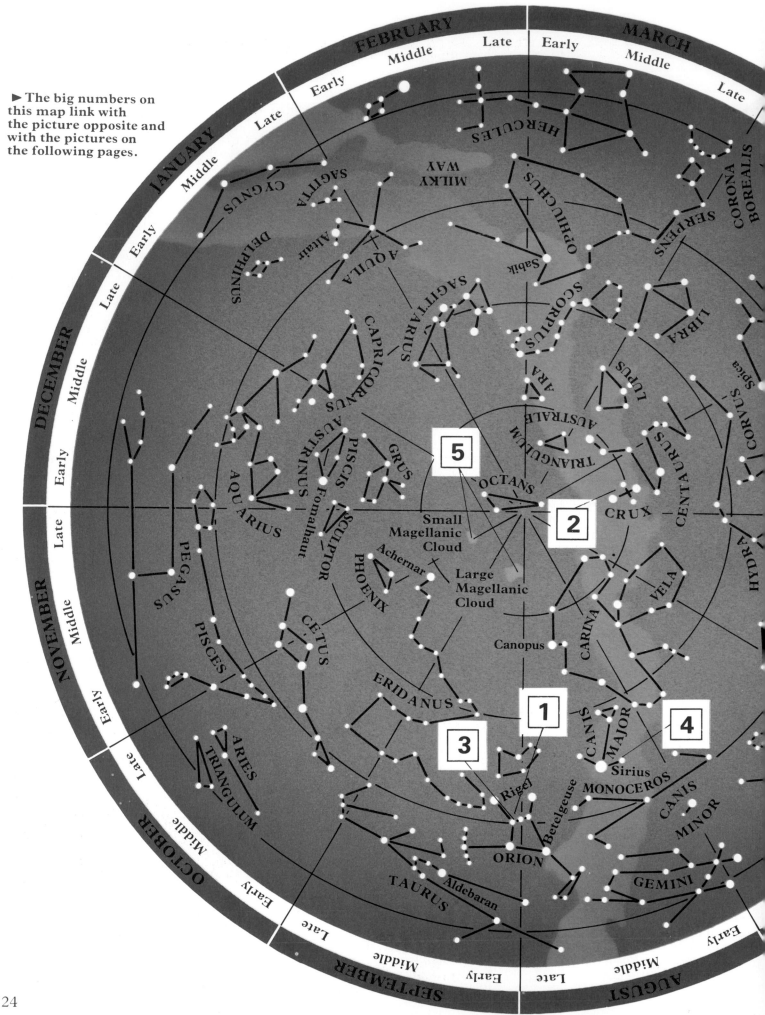

► The big numbers on this map link with the picture opposite and with the pictures on the following pages.

FEBRUARY

MARCH

Late

Early

Middle

Early

Middle

Late

Late

JANUARY

Middle

CYGNUS

SAGITTA

MILKY WAY

HERCULES

CORONA BOREALIS

Early

DELPHINUS

Altair

AQUILA

OPHIUCHUS

SERPENS

Late

DECEMBER

Early

CAPRICORNUS

SAGITTARIUS

Sabik

SCORPIUS

LIBRA

Spica

Middle

AQUARIUS

PISCIS AUSTRINUS

CAPRICORNUS

GRUS

ARA

TRIANGULUM AUSTRALE

LUPUS

CORVUS

Late

Fomalhaut

SCULPTOR

5

OCTANS

CRUX

CENTAURUS

HYDRA

Middle

PEGASUS

PISCIS AUSTRINUS

PHOENIX

Small Magellanic Cloud

2

VELA

NOVEMBER

Early

Achernar

Large Magellanic Cloud

CARINA

PISCES

CETUS

ERIDANUS

Canopus

Late

TRIANGULUM

ARIES

3

1

CANIS MAJOR

4

OCTOBER

Middle

Rigel

Betelgeuse

Sirius

MONOCEROS

CANIS MINOR

Early

ORION

GEMINI

Late

TAURUS

Aldebaran

Early

SEPTEMBER

Middle

Early

Late

Middle

Early

AUGUST

Star-spotting in the southern sky

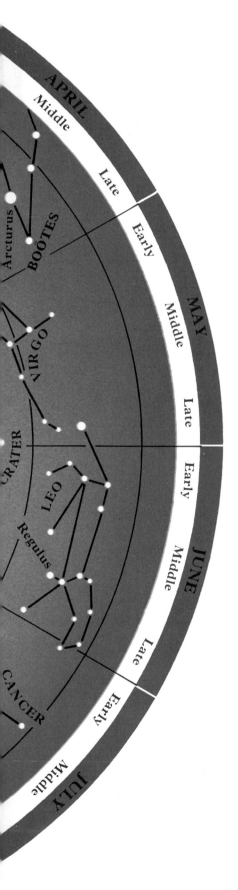

The stars shown on this map can be seen from all the inhabited regions of the southern hemisphere. The stars around the outer edges belong to the northern sky, but at the right times of year they can be seen low on the horizon.

The Greek alphabet is used to name stars. In each constellation one star — usually the brightest — is called Alpha (the first letter), the next Beta (the second letter) and so on. Then comes a slightly altered form of the constellation name. Thus Alpha Centauri is the brightest star in Centaurus.

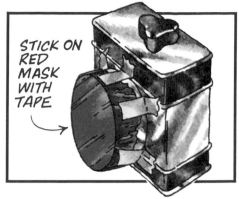

STICK ON RED MASK WITH TAPE →

▲ You will need a nightlight to read with whenever you take your sky map outside to go star spotting. So that the glare does not spoil your night vision, take along a torch masked with red cellophane.

Wonders of the southern sky

Because the southern sky was neglected for so long, a number of surprises awaited astronomers when they directed their attentions here. In the constellation Centaurus they found our closest stellar neighbour. Proxima Centauri is a small dim red star just 4.2 light years away. Here in the south are also the nearest galaxies, called the Magellanic Clouds after their discoverer, Ferdinand Magellan.

▲ Hanging near the three stars forming the 'belt' of Orion is one of the most magnificent sights in the sky. To the naked eye, the Great Nebula is a faint fuzzy patch. Seen through a telescope, as shown in the picture above, it leaps into view as a vast and colourful cloud of gas 16 light years across.

The young hot stars embedded in the cloud radiate 8 times as brightly as the Sun. They make the billowing clouds of surrounding gas heat up and shine as well.

▲ The Southern Cross, shown in close-up above, is a tiny constellation, the smallest in the sky: Two of its member stars point toward the south, just as two of The Plough's stars point north toward Polaris.

▲ Dark nebulae are clouds of cold dust and gases. They can only be seen when they blot out part of a lighter background of stars. The Horsehead Nebula in Orion, shown above, stands out in silhouette against the bright stars behind.

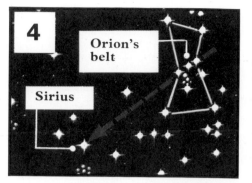

▲ Sirius is the brightest star in the southern night sky. It is also known as the Dog Star because it lies in the constellation Canis Major, the Great Dog. The picture above shows you how to find Sirius using Orion's Belt as a guide.

Plans for your sky-spy

This simple gadget will show you which stars can be seen from your home at any particular time of the year.

Get a large sheet of tracing paper and lay it over this page. Trace off the solid black lines from the yellow half-plan on the right. Now mark on the time arrows from midnight to 6 am.

Flip the tracing paper over. Trace out the other half of the plan. Mark on the evening time arrows from midnight to 6 pm. Also trace on the star where the vertical and horizontal lines cross.

Slide the star on your tracing paper along the degrees of latitude scale until it rests on your own latitude. You can find the latitude of your home in an atlas.

Here are some examples:

Copenhagen	56 North
London	52 North
Munich	48 North
Rome	42 North
Rio de Janeiro	23 South
Sydney	34 South

Now trace out the dotted oval of the horizon line. As you can see, the oval moves north or south depending on where you live.

Transfer your finished tracing onto a sheet of stiff card cut out to the same shape. Lastly, cut out the oval centre. Your Sky-Spy is now complete.

← MIDNIGHT

MORNING TIME ARROWS

STAR

EVENING TIME ARROWS

← TRACING PAPER

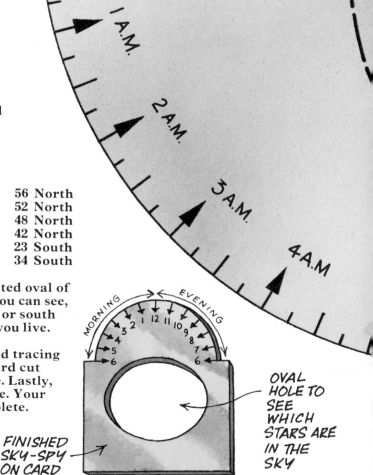

12 MID-NIGHT

1 A.M.

2 A.M.

3 A.M.

4 A.M

MORNING   EVENING

FINISHED SKY-SPY ON CARD

OVAL HOLE TO SEE WHICH STARS ARE IN THE SKY

5

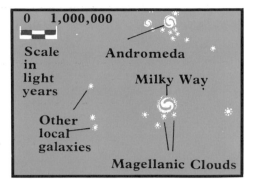

▲ The Magellanic Clouds were first noted in 1521. They are visible only in the southern sky. The Large Cloud, also known by its scientific name Nubecula Major, is shown in the picture above. It is 170,000 light years away from the Milky Way making it the nearest galaxy to us, almost a satellite in fact. It is 23,000 light years across. Unlike spiral and disc-shaped galaxies, the clouds have no particular shape or form. They are classed as irregular galaxies.

▲ The Magellanic Clouds and 30 other galaxies belong to the Local Group. This cluster of galaxies (of which the Milky Way is a member) lies within a 5 million light year diameter sphere. Other clusters can contain up to 2,500 galaxies.

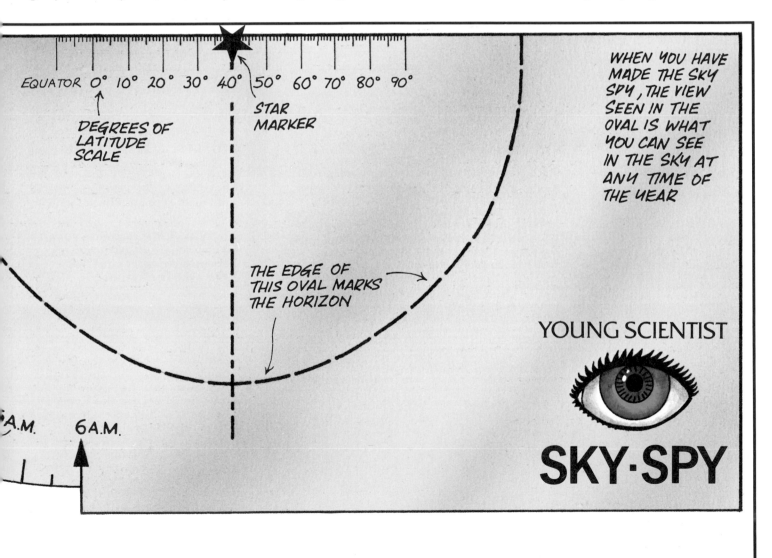

Equator 0° 10° 20° 30° 40° 50° 60° 70° 80° 90°

DEGREES OF LATITUDE SCALE

STAR MARKER

THE EDGE OF THIS OVAL MARKS THE HORIZON

WHEN YOU HAVE MADE THE SKY SPY, THE VIEW SEEN IN THE OVAL IS WHAT YOU CAN SEE IN THE SKY AT ANY TIME OF THE YEAR

A.M. 6A.M.

YOUNG SCIENTIST

SKY·SPY

Other things to see

Meteors

At regular times of the year, swarms of meteors cross the Earth's orbit. A heavy meteor shower looks like lots of streaks of light coming from a point in the sky — the radiant.

Name of shower	Where to look	When to look
Aquarids	SW of Pegasus	May 4-6
Geminids	Castor in Gemini	December 11-14
Leonids	Leo	November 16-18
Lyrids	Between Hercules and Vega	April 20-22
Orionids	Between Orion and Gemini	October 18-22
Perseids	Perseus	August 10-14
Quadran-tids	Between Boötes and Draco	January 2-4
Taurids	Between Taurus and Perseus	November 5-9

Man-made satellites

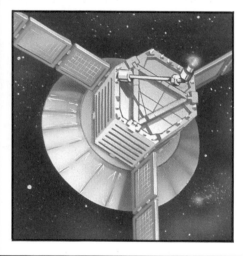

Some of the most successful satellites have been orbiting astronomical observatories, such as COBE (Cosmic Background Explorer), shown here. It was launched to study microwave radiation, left over from the Big Bang, that fills the universe. Other satellites observe infra-red, ultra-violet and X-rays from space, which cannot penetrate Earth's atmosphere. Other types of satellite 'look' at the Earth – to observe the weather, locate resources, relay TV and phone messages, or spy on armed forces.

Comets

Comets travel in long swooping orbits that may take them far into the outer reaches of the solar system. It can be hundreds, even thousands of years before they return.

ENCKE'S: Appears at a regular interval of 3.3 years. This small comet swings as far as Jupiter before turning back to the Sun. Visible only with a telescope.

HALLEY'S: Shown above, this comet returns every 76 years. It last appeared in 1986, when five space probes flew by it to make observations.

HUMASON 1961E: Discovered in 1961, this large comet has a long flat orbit that takes thousands of years to complete. It is next expected in the year 4860.

IKEYA-SEKI: Discovered in 1965 by two amateur astronomers, this bright comet could be seen even in daytime.

Eclipses

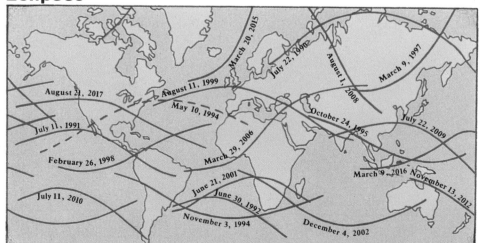

Solar eclipses occur when the Moon passes between the Earth and the Sun, and the Moon's shadow races across the Earth at speeds up to 3,500 kph. On each of the 'paths of totality' shown here, the eclipse is total — the main disc of the Sun is completely blocked out. On each side of the path a partial eclipse can be seen, in which the Moon only partly covers the Sun. The dotted line marks the path of an annular eclipse, in which the Moon is at its farthest from the Earth and the rim of the Sun appears around the Moon's edge.

Strange frontiers

Recently discovered objects in space are stranger than any astronomer had predicted. Scientists know that gravity is the weakest force in the universe, yet they were astonished to find that it can sometimes make matter and energy apparently vanish.

A place where this occurs is called a black hole. In this region, the forces of gravity are so intense that anything which comes near is sucked inside. Even light rays cannot escape its clutches, so a black hole is completely invisible!

Birth of a black hole

Black holes are the result of a process called gravitational collapse. The atoms of a star are squeezed closer and closer to each other so that the star gets ever more dense — a little like the difference between say, balsa wood and lead. One way in which this could happen is when a giant star, shown on the right, explodes violently.

1

The outer layers of the star are flung off into space. If there is enough material left in the core, it collapses inward to form a small super-dense globe called a neutron star. A single matchbox of it would weigh 10,000 million tonnes. A neutron star sends out beams of radiation that swing round like lighthouse beams as the star spins.

2

Some neutron stars shrink still further to become black holes. A black hole is an odd object — incredibly small, yet enormously dense. The picture below shows how a black hole bends the fabric of space, creating a sort of 'plug-hole' effect. Anything falling inside it is likely, as far as astronomers can tell, to be completely crushed or sucked right out of our universe.

3

A world the size of a pea!

If the Earth were crushed as much as the matter inside a black hole, it would fit inside a sphere the size of a pea. From where you read these words, the force of the black hole's gravity would pull you to pieces and swallow you into the page.

Sky firsts

Hundreds of notable landmarks lie scattered through the history of astronomy. Below are just a very few.

140 AD
Ptolemy of Alexandria wrote the Almagest, recording all the astronomical knowledge of the ancient world. He also produced the most accurate star catalogue of his time.

1054 AD
Chinese astronomers recorded a supernova explosion in Taurus. The Crab Nebula is the remnant of this event.

1543
Copernicus laid the groundwork of modern astronomy by showing that the Earth and all the planets revolved around the Sun.

Isaac Newton's reflecting telescope

1608
The Dutchman, Hans Lippershey, used the magnifying power of glass lenses to build the first telescope. The following year, Galileo used his own telescope to observe sunspots, the moons of Jupiter and the stars of the Milky Way.

1671
The first telescopes were crude refractors. In 1671, Newton invented the reflecting telescope. Though only 16 cm long, it was as powerful as a 200 cm refractor.

1937
Grote Reber built the first true radio telescope. He set up a 9 m reflecting dish in his garden to study the radio noises that came from the sky.

1960
Radio astronomers discover quasars (quasi-stellar radio sources). These puzzling objects lie at tremendous distances from us—as much as 15,000 million light years away. They are a fraction the size of galaxies yet hundreds of times brighter.

1967
Unexpected signals from space were discovered by astronomers at Cambridge, England. These unknown pulses turned out to be coming from rapidly spinning neutron stars. They were called pulsars. One has been found in the middle of the Crab Nebula, right at the heart of the supernova explosion of 1054.

1987
In a small nearby galaxy, the Large Magellanic Cloud, a blue supergiant star blew up. This supernova, as an exploding star is called, was 160,000 light years away, and was the nearest to the Earth since the telescope was invented.

1990
The Hubble Space Telescope, with a 2.4-m mirror, was launched into orbit. There were errors in manufacture that would take years to correct, but then it will search for other solar systems and help to measure the size of the universe.

Crab Nebula

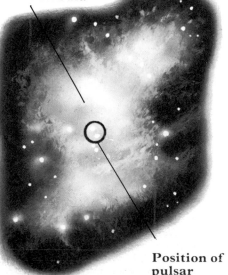

Position of pulsar

Sky facts

People have been studying the sky for centuries, yet it never ceases to yield new secrets.

In the last 40 years, radio astronomy has opened up a new side of the universe. Astronomers no longer study only visible light. They can now explore nearly the whole spectrum of radiation. Their findings are proving to be more spectacular than anyone could have imagined.

Here is a list of the ten brightest stars you can see in the sky.

Name	Constellation
Sirius	Canis Major
Canopus	Carina
Alpha Centauri	Centaurus
Arcturus	Boötes
Vega	Lyra
Capella	Auriga
Rigel	Orion
Procyon	Canis Minor
Achernar	Eridanus
Beta Centauri	Centaurus

Although the face of Venus is hidden by an unbroken layer of cloud, the surface is not so dark as was expected. The USSR landed Venus 9 and 10 successfully in 1975. The probes sent back pictures that show the surface to be no gloomier than an overcast day time scene on Earth. Venusian clouds proved to be more like a haze than a blanket.

Quasars are the most energetic objects in the sky, radiating the energy of 100,000 million Suns from compact regions not much bigger than our own solar system. They are explosions at the centres of giant galaxies, probably occurring in a ring of hot gases circling a very heavy black hole. They are also the most distant objects yet discovered, some lying about 15,000 million light years away.

The Sun shivers, but not with cold. Astronomers have recently detected wobbling movements that make the Sun larger or smaller by up to 10 km. At present, astronomers have no idea what causes them.

Pluto is really a double planet—its moon Charon is almost half as large as Pluto itself. Its strange orbit brings the Pluto-Charon double planet closer to the Sun than Neptune between 1979 and 1999. Pluto itself is the smallest planet in the solar system. It is only three-quarters the size of Mercury and is probably made of solid frozen methane (natural gas).

Astronomers estimate that there could be up to 10 million black holes in the Milky Way galaxy.

Time-exposure photograph of a man-made satellite passing overhead. If you see one, it will look like a bright moving star.

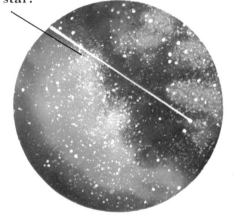

Massive galaxies can act as giant lenses, distorting quasars lying beyond them and even making them look double. The matter we can see in the universe is probably only about 10 percent of what is really present. The 'dark' matter may consist of faint dwarf stars, intergalactic gas, or subatomic particles filling space.
Dust clouds that are probably a solar system in the making have been observed around several stars, such as Beta Pictoris.

Sky words

This glossary includes words that are not fully explained elsewhere in the book.

The spectrum

Radio waves · Infrared waves · Visible light · Ultraviolet rays · X-rays · Gamma rays

Astronomical unit (AU)
The average distance from the Sun to the Earth (150 million km) is an astronomical unit. It is a shorthand way of measuring distances within the solar system.

Big bang
Theory which holds that the entire universe began as a vast 'super-atom' of matter and energy that exploded, (the Bang), and sent all the galaxies hurtling through space.

Binary
Two stars in the same sun-system revolving around each other. Three, four and even more stars can link together like this.

Constellation
Group of stars seeming to make a shape or pattern in the sky.

Cosmic rays
Ultra high speed atomic particles that come shooting to Earth from outer space and from the Sun.

Galaxy
Stars are not randomly sprinkled throughout the universe. They are grouped in great clouds or galaxies. Each one contains thousands of millions of stars.

Gravity
The force of attraction that exists between one heavenly body and another. The more massive an object, the greater its gravity.

Light year
The distance light travels in a year (9,460,000 million km).

Magnitude
The brightness of a star or other object shining in space.

Orbit
The path of one body as it moves around another one in space. The pull of gravity keeps objects in orbit.

Radiation
Electromagnetic energy, whose full range comprises the spectrum described below.

Red shift
When the light of a star shifts to the red end of the spectrum, the star is receding from us. This is an example of the Doppler Effect.

Satellite
Smaller objects which revolve around a larger one and are held by its gravity are called satellites. The Moon is a satellite of Earth.

Spectrum
Visible light is one kind of radiation. Radio waves, infrared, ultraviolet and X-rays are other kinds. The entire range of radiation is called the spectrum. Visible light takes up a very small slot somewhere in the middle.

Solar wind
Clouds of atomic particles streaming away from the Sun at high speed.

Index

Going further

Organizations

BAYS
(British Association Youth Section)
Fortress House
23 Savile Row
London, W.1

British Astronomical Association
Burlington House
Piccadilly
London, W.1

Junior Astronomical Society
35 Fairway
Keyworth, Nottingham

Books to read

Spotter's Guide to the Night Sky
by Nigel Henbest
Usborne, 1985

The Greenwich Guide to Stargazing
Carole Stott
George Philip, 1987

The Greenwich Guide to the Planets
Stuart Malin
George Philip, 1987

The Sky at Night
by Patrick Moore
Harrap, 1989

The Monthly Sky Guide
by Ian Ridpath and Will Tirion
Cambridge University Press, 1990

The Skywatcher's Handbook
edited by Colin Ronan
Corgi, 1985